a Little Golden Book® Collection

Sleepytime Tales

A GOLDEN BOOK • NEW YORK

A GOLDEN BOOK • NEW YORK

Contents

The POKY LITTLE PUPPY

FIVE little puppies dug a hole under the fence and went for a walk in the wide, wide world.

Through the meadow they went, down the road, over the bridge, across the green grass, and up the hill, one after the other.

And when they got to the top of the hill, they counted themselves: one, two, three, four. One little puppy wasn't there.

"Now where in the world is that poky little puppy?" they wondered. For he certainly wasn't on top of the hill.

He wasn't going down the other side. The only thing they could see going down was a fuzzy caterpillar.

He wasn't coming up this side. The only thing they could see coming up was a quick green lizard.

But when they looked down at the grassy place near the bottom of the hill, there he was, running round and round, his nose to the ground.

"What is he doing?" the four little puppies asked one another. And down they went to see, roly-poly, pell-mell, tumble-bumble, till they came to the green grass; and there they stopped short.

"What in the world are you doing?" they asked.

"I smell something!" said the poky little puppy.

Then the four little puppies began to sniff, and they smelled it, too.

"Rice pudding!" they said.

And home they went, as fast as they could go, over the bridge, up the road, through the meadow, and under the fence. And there, sure enough, was dinner waiting for them, with rice pudding for dessert.

But their mother was greatly displeased. "So you're the little puppies who dig holes under fences!" she said. "No rice pudding tonight!" And she made them go straight to bed.

But the poky little puppy came home after everyone was sound asleep.

He ate up the rice pudding and crawled into bed as happy as a lark.

The next morning someone had filled the hole and put up a sign. The sign said:

BUT. . . . .

The five little puppies dug a hole under the fence, just the same, and went for a walk in the wide, wide world.

Through the meadow they went, down the road, over the bridge, across the green grass, and up the hill, two and two. And when they got to the top of the hill, they counted themselves: one, two, three, four. One little puppy wasn't there.

"Now where in the world is that poky little puppy?" they wondered. For he certainly wasn't on top of the hill.

He wasn't going down the other side. The only thing they could see going down was a big black spider.

He wasn't coming up this side. The only thing
they could see coming up was a brown hop-toad.

But when they looked down at the grassy
place near the bottom of the hill, there was

the poky little puppy, sitting still as a stone, with his head on one side and his ears cocked up.

"What is he doing?" the four little puppies asked one another. And down they went to see, roly-poly, pell-mell, tumble-bumble, till they came to the green grass; and there they stopped short.

"What in the world are you doing?" they asked.

"I hear something!" said the poky little puppy.

The four little puppies listened, and they could hear it, too. "Chocolate custard!" they cried. "Someone is spooning it into our bowls!"

And home they went as fast as they could go, over the bridge, up the road, through the meadow, and under the fence. And there, sure enough, was dinner waiting for them, with chocolate custard for dessert.

But their mother was greatly displeased. "So you're the little puppies who will dig holes under fences!" she said. "No chocolate custard tonight!" And she made them go straight to bed.

But the poky little puppy came home after everyone else was sound asleep, and

he ate up all the chocolate custard and crawled into bed as happy as a lark.

The next morning someone had filled the hole and put up a sign.

The sign said:

DON'T EVER **EVER** DIG HOLES UNDER THIS FENCE!

BUT...

In spite of that, the five little puppies dug a hole under the fence and went for a walk in the wide, wide world.

Through the meadow they went, down the road, over the bridge, across the green grass, and up the hill, two and two. And when they got to the top of the hill, they counted themselves: one, two, three, four. One little puppy wasn't there.

"Now where in the world is that poky little puppy?" they wondered. For he certainly wasn't on top of the hill.

He wasn't going down the other side. The only thing they could see going down was a little grass snake.

He wasn't coming up this side. The only thing
they could see coming up was a big grasshopper.

But when they looked down at the grassy place near the bottom of the hill, there he was, looking hard at something on the ground in front of him.

"What is he doing?" the four little puppies asked one another. And down they went to see, roly-poly, pell-mell, tumble-bumble, till they came to the green grass; and there they stopped short.

"What in the world are you doing?" they asked.

"I see something!" said the poky little puppy.

The four little puppies looked, and they could see it, too. It was a ripe, red strawberry growing there in the grass.

"Strawberry shortcake!" they cried.

And home they went as fast as they could go, over the bridge, up the road, through the meadow, and under the fence. And there, sure enough, was dinner waiting for them, with strawberry shortcake for dessert.

But their mother said: "So you're the little puppies who dug that hole under the fence again! No strawberry shortcake for supper tonight!" And she made them go straight to bed.

But the four little puppies waited till they thought she was asleep, and then they slipped out and filled up the hole, and when they turned around, there was their mother watching them.

"What good little puppies!" she said. "Come have some strawberry shortcake!"

And this time, when the poky little puppy got home, he had to squeeze in through a wide place in the fence. And there were his four brothers and sisters, licking the last crumbs from their saucer.

"Dear me!" said his mother. "What a pity you're so poky! Now the strawberry shortcake is all gone!"

So the poky little puppy had to go to bed without a single bite of shortcake, and he felt very sorry for himself.

And the next morning someone had put up a sign that read:

NO DESSERTS EVER UNLESS PUPPIES NEVER DIG HOLES UNDER THIS FENCE AGAIN!

Baby Dear is my brand-new baby doll.
Daddy brought her to me on a very special day.

It was the day he brought Mommy and
our new baby home from the hospital.

Mommy loves her baby.
And I love mine.

We give our babies their bottles.

Then we pat their backs
to bubble them.

Mommy changes her baby.

And I change mine.

Mommy bathes her baby.
And I bathe Baby Dear.

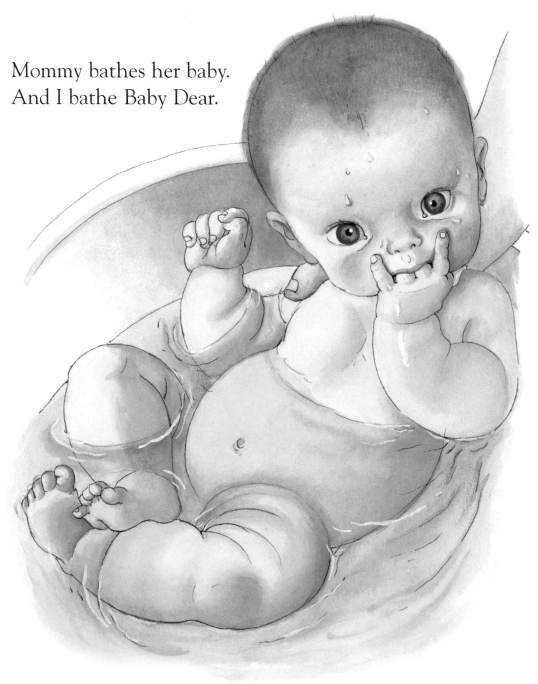

We play Little Piggy
with their little pink toes.

We dress our babies in their bonnets before we take
them out.

Mommy has a carriage for her baby. And I have one
for Baby Dear.

We go walking together with our babies.

Mommy's baby sleeps in the little white bed
that used to be mine.
My baby sleeps in a cradle all her own.

Mommy has a book
for her baby and I have one
for Baby Dear.

We write things in our books about our babies.

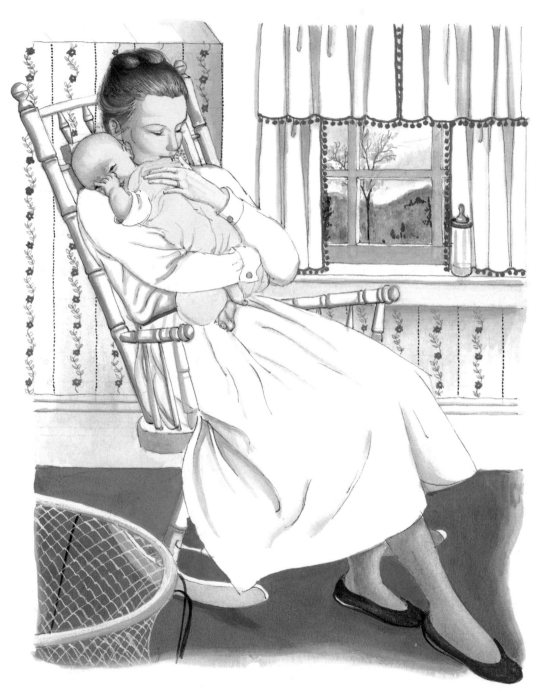

Mommy sings to her baby and I sing to mine.

We smile at our babies and talk to them.
Mommy says this is the way our babies know
they are the most wonderful babies in the world.

Sometimes Mommy lets me hold her baby.
Mommy's baby is my baby sister.

When my baby sister is a big girl
I will let her hold Baby Dear.

THE COLOR KITTENS

Once there were two color kittens with green eyes, Brush and Hush. They liked to mix and make colors by splashing one color into another. They had buckets and buckets

and buckets and buckets of color to splash
around with. Out of these colors they would
make all the colors in the world.

The buckets had the colors written on them, but of course the kittens couldn't read. They had to tell by the colors. "It is very easy," said Brush. "Red is red. Blue is blue," said Hush.

But they had no green. "No green paint!" said Brush and Hush. And they wanted green paint, of course, because nearly every place they liked to go was green.

Green as cats' eyes
Green as grass
By streams of water
Green as glass.

So they tried to make some green paint.

Brush mixed red paint and white paint together—and what did that make? It didn't make green.

RED

WHITE

But it made pink.

Pink as pigs

Pink as toes

A PIG

ROSE A

Pink as a rose
Or a baby's nose.

Then Hush mixed yellow and red
together, and it made orange.

Orange as an orange tree

Orange as a bumblebee

Orange as the setting sun
Sinking slowly in the sea.

The kittens were delighted, but it didn't make green.

Then they mixed red and blue together—and what did that make? It didn't make green. It made a deep dark purple.

Purple as violets

Purple as prunes

Purple as shadows
On late afternoons.

Still no green! And then . . .

O wonderful kittens! O Brush! O Hush!

At last, almost by accident, the kittens poured a bucket of blue and a bucket of yellow together, and it came to pass that they made a green as green as grass.

Green as green leaves on a tree

Green as islands in the sea.

The little kittens were so happy with all the colors they had made that they began to paint everything around them. They painted . . .

Green leaves
  and red berries

and purple flowers
  and pink cherries

Red tables
  and yellow chairs

Black trees
  with golden pears.

Then the kittens got so excited they knocked their buckets upside down and all the colors ran together. Yellow, red, a little blue, and a little black . . . and that made brown.

Brown as a tugboat

Brown as an old goat

Brown as a beaver

BROWN

And in all that brown, the sun went down.
It was evening and the colors began to
disappear in the warm dark night.

The kittens fell asleep in the warm dark
night with all their colors out of sight and as
they slept they dreamed their dream —

A wonderful dream
Of a red rose tree
That turned all white
When you counted three

One . . . Two . . .

Three

Of a purple land
In a pale pink sea

Where apples fell
From a golden tree

And then a world of Easter eggs
That danced about on little short legs.

And they dreamed that
A green cat danced
With a little pink dog

Till they all disappeared in a soft gray fog.

And suddenly Brush woke up and Hush woke up. It was morning. They crawled out of bed into a big bright world. The sky was wild with sunshine.

The kittens were wild with purring and pouncing—

Pounce

Pounce

Pounce

They got so pouncy they knocked over the
buckets and all the colors ran out together.

There were all the colors in the world and
the color kittens had made them.

GOOD NIGHT, LITTLE BEAR

It is time for Little Bear to go to bed.
Mother Bear closes the storybook.
She gives Little Bear a good-night kiss.

Then over to
his big furry father
runs the little bear.

Wheee!

Father Bear swings his little one high up
to his shoulders for a ride to bed.

"Duck your head," calls Mother Bear, just in time.
And into the snug little bedroom they go.

Squeak!
The tiny bed sighs as Father Bear sits down.
"Now, into bed with you," he says.
He waits for Little Bear to climb down.
But Little Bear doesn't move.
He sits up on his father's shoulders and grins.
Father Bear waits. He yawns a rumbly yawn.
Is Father Bear falling asleep?
No. Suddenly he opens his eyes again.

"Why, I must have been dreaming,"
says Father Bear, pretending to wake up.
But what's this?
There is no furry head on the pillow.
Where can Little Bear be?
Father Bear looks under the pillow.
Nobody there.
He doesn't seem to feel
something tickling his ear.

Aha.
There's a lump down under the blanket.
Father Bear pats the lump.
But it doesn't squeak or wiggle.
Can it be Little Bear?

Why, it's the toy teddy and the blue bunny
waiting for Little Bear to come to bed!

"Mother, that naughty bear is hiding,"
says Father Bear to Mother Bear, with
a wink.
"Maybe he's hiding under the kitchen stove,"
says Mother Bear, who loves a joke.

Bang! Bang!
Father Bear rattles the pots and pans
on top of the stove.
"Little Bear, I'm coming to get you!" he roars.

Father Bear reaches under the stove.
He feels something soft and furry.
Is it Little Bear?

No.
It's only Father Bear's old winter mitten.

'Way up high Little Bear claps his paw
to his mouth. But not in time.
"I heard that Little Bear laugh," says Father.
"Now where can he be hiding?"

"Is he standing outside the front door?
I'll turn the knob softly—
and fling the door wide!"
No. There are no bears out there.
Just a family of fat little rabbits
nibbling lettuce in the garden.
"Shoo!" snorts Father Bear.

"Something is hiding in the woodbox,"
whispers Mother Bear.
"Creep over there on tip toe,
and you may catch a little bear."
Eeek!
There's just a wee mouse hiding there.

There's nobody up high, on the china shelf.
"Ouch!"
Little Bear bumps his head.
"Who said Ouch?" asks Father Bear.
"Mother, did you say Ouch?"
"Not I," smiles Mother Bear.
Oh she is a tease.

"Now where is that naughty bear hiding?
He wouldn't run away.
Not a little bear who is always hungry
for chocolate cake."
And that big Daddy Bear cuts himself a huge piece
of chocolate cake right under the little bear's nose.

Little Bear suddenly feels hungry.
But just then Father Bear stops smack
in front of the mirror.
"Why, there he is," roars the big bear.
"But you couldn't find me," squeaks Little Bear,
reaching for chocolate cake.

Wheee!
Off Daddy's shoulders and down to the sofa.
Bounce. Bounce. Bounce.
"Wasn't that a good hiding place, Mommy?
No one could find me up there."

"But I've found you now," says Father Bear.
Little Bear wiggles and giggles under his Daddy's
strong arm . . . all the way into bed.

"Did I really fool you, Daddy?"
asks Little Bear.
Father Bear just laughs and winks.
Do you think Father Bear knew all the time?

THE WONDERFUL HOUSE

Who lives here?

A boy and a girl live here.

But who lives here?

A horse, of course, lives here.

And who lives here?

Two little birds that fly in the air live here.

But who in the world lives here!

A big fat turtle.
He lives here.

And who lives here?

A slow little snail.
And wherever he goes, his house goes, too.

But who lives here?

A big old lion and his lion family.
They live here.

And who lives here?

A nutty little squirrel. He lives here.

And who lives here?

Bow wow wow.
A dog lives here.
Bow wow wow.
Bow wow. Meow.

But who lives here?
Deep in the dark mysterious river.

I live here. My dear!

But who in the world lives in here?

A funny little rabbit.
He lives here.

Who lives here? And who lives there?
But what is that flying through the air!

Bees, stop your buzzing! Who comes there?

What oh what is this? And who lives there?
In that roly-poly place that floats in the air?

Far away, it is coming near.
Still far away, it will soon be here.

What in the world! It flies through the air.
Old owl, tell us, who lives there?

Is it a circus clown? Does he live there?
In that winged house up in the air?

No! He lives in a tent with a big pair of shoes.
It is not a clown. It is not a clown.

Is it a wild elephant? Does he live there?
In that wonderful house that flies through the air?

No!

A big wild elephant lives under the sun
And the moon and the stars, under a tree.
It is not a wild elephant up in the air.

Is it a curious monkey?
Does he live there?

It is not a curious monkey. But see him stare
At what is coming through the air.

A giant sees it.
Does he live there?

No! Certainly not!

And now you guess whose house is there,
Coming nearer through the air.

Is it a walrus's house?

Or a lobster's house?

Or a frog's house?

Or a witch's house?

Or a piggywig's house?

Is it a giraffe's house?

Or a fish's house?

Or a hat's house?

Or a dog biscuit's house?

No! All guesses are wrong.
It is a wonderful house

With wings to fly with
And wheels to roll on
And pontoons to float on
And balloons to hang on
And flowers in the windows

And a boy and a girl live in this house
With a dog and a rabbit and a cat and a mouse
And animals everywhere.
And they all go flying through the air,
To where they want to go.

THE WHISPERING RABBIT

O<small>NCE</small> there was a sleepy little rabbit
Who began to yawn—
And he yawned and he yawned and he yawned
and he yawned,
"Hmmm————"

He opened his little rabbit mouth when he yawned till you could see his white front teeth and his little round pink mouth, and he yawned and he yawned until suddenly a bee flew into his mouth and he swallowed the bee.

"Hooo—hooo—," said a fat old owl. "Always keep your paw in front of your mouth when you yawn," hooted the owl.

"Rabbits never do that," said the sleepy little rabbit.

"Silly rabbits!" said the owl, and he flew away.

The little rabbit was just calling after him, but when the little rabbit opened his mouth to speak, the bumblebee had curled up to sleep in his throat——AND——all he could do was whisper.

"What shall I do?" he whispered to a squirrel who wasn't sleepy.

"Wake him up," said the squirrel. "Wake up the bumblebee."

"How?" whispered the rabbit. "All I can do is whisper and I'm sleepy and I want to go to sleep and who can sleep with a bumblebee—"

Suddenly a wise old groundhog popped up out of the ground.

"All I can do is whisper," said the little rabbit.

"All the better," said the groundhog.

"Come here, little rabbit," he said, "and I will whisper to you how to wake up a bumblebee.

"You have to make the littlest noise that you can possibly make because a bumblebee doesn't bother about big noises. He is a very little bee and he is only interested in little noises."

"Like a loud whisper?" asked the rabbit.

"Too loud," said the groundhog, and popped back into his hole.

"A little noise," whispered the rabbit, and he started making little rabbit noises—he made a noise as quiet as the sound of a bird's wing cutting the air, but the bee didn't wake up. So the little rabbit made the sound of snow falling, but the bee didn't wake up.

So the little rabbit made the sound of a bug
breathing and a fly sneezing and grass rustling and a
fireman thinking. Still the bee didn't wake up. So the
rabbit sat and thought of all the little sounds he
could think of—What could they be?

A sound quiet as snow melting, quiet as a flower growing, quiet as an egg, quiet as—And suddenly he knew the little noise that he would make—and he made it.

It was like a little click made hundreds of miles away by a bumblebee in an apple tree in full bloom on a mountaintop. It was the very small click of a bee swallowing some honey from an apple blossom.

And at that the bee woke up.

He thought he was missing something and away
he flew.

And then what did the little rabbit do? That sleepy
sleepy little rabbit?

He closed his mouth
He closed his eyes
He closed his ears
And he tucked in his paws
And twitched his nose
And he went sound asleep!

GOING TO SLEEP

ALL over the world the animals are going to sleep—the birds and the bees, the horse, the butterfly, and the cat.

In their high nests by the ocean, the fish hawks are going to sleep. And how does a young fish hawk go to sleep? The same as any other bird in the world.

She folds her wings and pushes herself deep in the nest, looks around and blinks her eyes three times, takes one long last look over the ocean, then tucks her head under her wing and sleeps like a bird.

And the fish in the sea sleep in the darkened sea when the long green light of the sun is gone.

And they sleep like fish, with their eyes wide open in some quiet current of the sea.

And above and beyond under the stars on the land, all the little horses are going to sleep. Some stand up in the still-dark fields and some fold their legs under them and lie down. But they all go to sleep like horses.

Even the bees and the butterflies sleep when the moths begin to fly. And they sleep like bees and butterflies under a leaf or a stick or a stone, with folded wings and their eyes wide open. For fish and bees and butterflies and flies never close their shiny eyes.

And the old fat bear in the deep dark woods goes into his warm cave to sleep for the whole winter.

So do the groundhogs and the hedgehogs, the skunks and the black-eyed raccoons. They eat a lot, then sleep until spring, a long warm sleep.

The THREE BEARS

Once upon a time there were three bears—
a great big papa bear, a middle-sized mama
bear, and a wee little baby bear.
They lived in a little house in the forest.

They had three chairs—a great big chair for the papa bear, a middle-sized chair for the mama bear, and a wee little chair for the baby bear.

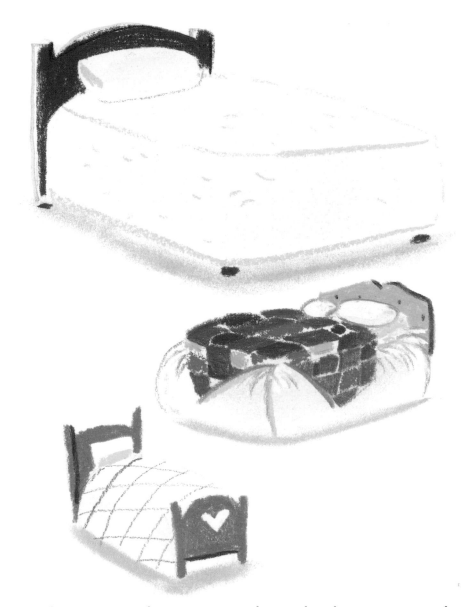

And upstairs there were three beds—a great big bed for the papa bear, a middle-sized bed for the mama bear, and a wee little bed for the baby bear.

One morning the mama bear made some
porridge for breakfast.

There was a great big bowl for the papa bear, a middle-sized bowl for the mama bear, and a wee little bowl for the baby bear.

But the porridge was too hot to eat, so the
three bears went out for a walk in the forest.

That same morning a little girl called Goldilocks was walking through the woods.

She came to the three bears' house. And she knocked on the door, but nobody called, "Come in." So she opened the door and went in.

Goldilocks saw the three chairs. She sat in the great big chair. It was too hard. The middle-sized chair was too soft. . . .

The baby chair was just right—but it broke
when she sat on it.

Now Goldilocks spied the porridge.

"I am hungry," she said.

So she tasted the porridge.

The porridge in the big bowl was too hot. The porridge in the middle-sized bowl was too cold. The porridge in the wee little bowl was just right—so she ate it all up.

Then Goldilocks went upstairs and tried the beds.

The great big bed was too hard.

The middle-sized bed was too soft.

But the wee little bed was oh, so nice! So
Goldilocks lay down and went to sleep.

Then home through the forest and back to their
house came the three bears—the great big bear,
the middle-sized bear, and the wee little baby bear.

The moment they stepped into the house, they saw that someone had been there.

"Humph!" said the papa bear in his great big voice. "Someone has been sitting in my chair!"

"Land sakes!" said the mama bear in her middle-sized voice. "Someone has been sitting in *my* chair."

"Oh, dear!" cried the baby bear in his wee little voice. "Someone has been sitting in *my* chair, and has broken it all to bits."

Then they all looked at the table.

"Humph," said the papa bear in his great big voice. "Someone has been tasting my porridge."

"And someone has been tasting *my* porridge," said the mama bear.

"Someone has eaten *my* porridge all up," said the baby bear sadly.

Then up the stairs went the three bears, with a thump–thump–thump, and a trot–trot–trot, and a skippity–skip–skip. (That was the wee little baby bear.)

"Humph," said the papa bear in his great big voice. "Someone has been sleeping in my bed!"

"And someone has been sleeping in *my* bed," said the mama bear.

"Oh, dear!" cried the baby bear in his wee little voice. "And someone has been sleeping in *my* bed, and here she is right now!"

Goldilocks opened her eyes and saw the three bears.

"Oh!" said Goldilocks.

She was so surprised that she jumped right out of the window and ran all the way home.

And she never saw the house in the forest again.

The Boy AND the Tigers

Once upon a time there was a little boy, and his name was Little Rajani. And his Mother was called Ramita. And his Father was called Kapaali. And Ramita made him a beautiful little Red Coat, and a pair of beautiful little Blue Trousers.

And Kapaali went to the Bazaar, and bought him
a beautiful Green Umbrella, and a lovely little pair of
Purple Shoes with Crimson Soles and Crimson Linings.

And then wasn't Little Rajani grand? So he put on all his Fine Clothes, and went out for a walk in the Jungle. And by and by he met a Tiger.

And the Tiger said to him, "Little Rajani, I'm going to eat you up!"

And Little Rajani said, "Oh! Please, Mr. Tiger, don't eat me up, and I'll give you my beautiful little Red Coat."

So the Tiger said, "Very well, I won't eat you this time, but you must give me your beautiful little Red Coat."

So the Tiger got poor Little Rajani's beautiful little
Red Coat, and went away saying, "Now I'm the grandest
Tiger in the Jungle."

And Little Rajani went on, and by and by he met
another Tiger, and it said to him, "Little Rajani, I'm going to
eat you up!"

And Little Rajani said, "Oh! Please, Mr. Tiger, don't eat me up, and I'll give you my beautiful little Blue Trousers."

So the Tiger said, "Very well, I won't eat you this time, but you must give me your beautiful little Blue Trousers."

So the Tiger got poor Little Rajani's beautiful little Blue Trousers, and went away saying, "Now *I'm* the grandest Tiger in the Jungle."

And Little Rajani went on and by and by he met another Tiger, and it said to him, "Little Rajani, I'm going to eat you up!"

And Little Rajani said, "Oh! Please, Mr. Tiger, don't eat me up, and I'll give you my beautiful little Purple Shoes with Crimson Soles and Crimson Linings."

But the Tiger said, "What use would your shoes be to me? I've got four feet, and you've got only two; you haven't got enough shoes for me."

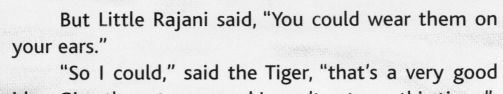

But Little Rajani said, "You could wear them on your ears."

"So I could," said the Tiger, "that's a very good idea. Give them to me, and I won't eat you this time."

So the Tiger got poor Little Rajani's beautiful little Purple Shoes with Crimson Soles and Crimson Linings, and went away saying, "Now *I'm* the grandest Tiger in the Jungle."

And by and by Little Rajani met another Tiger, and it said to him, "Little Rajani, I'm going to eat you up!"

And Little Rajani said, "Oh! Please, Mr. Tiger, don't eat me up, and I'll give you my beautiful Green Umbrella."

But the Tiger said, "How can I carry an umbrella, when I need all my paws for walking with?"

"You could tie a knot on your tail and carry it that way," said Little Rajani.

"So I could," said the Tiger. "Give it to me, and I won't eat you this time."

So he got poor Little Rajani's beautiful Green Umbrella, and went away saying, "Now *I'm* the grandest Tiger in the Jungle."

And poor Little Rajani went away crying, because the cruel Tigers had taken all his fine clothes.

Presently he heard a horrible noise that sounded like "Gr-r-r-r-r-rrrrrrr," and it got louder and louder. "Oh! Dear!" said Little Rajani. "There are all the Tigers coming back to eat me up! What shall I do?"

So he ran quickly to a palm tree, and peeped round it to see what the matter was.

And there he saw all the Tigers fighting, and disputing which of them was the grandest. And at last they all got so angry that they jumped up and took off all the fine clothes, and began to tear each other with their claws, and bite each other with their great big white teeth.

And they came rolling and tumbling right to the foot of the very tree where Little Rajani was hiding, but he jumped quickly in behind the umbrella. And the Tigers all caught hold of each other's tails, as they wrangled and scrambled, and so they found themselves in a ring round the tree.

Then, when the Tigers were very wee and very far away, Little Rajani jumped up, and called out, "Oh! Tigers! Why have you taken off all your nice clothes? Don't you want them anymore?"

But the Tigers only answered, "Gr-r-rrrr!"

Then Little Rajani said, "If you want them, say so, or I'll take them away."

But the Tigers would not let go of each other's tails, and so they could only say, "Gr-r-r-r-rrrrrr!"

So Little Rajani put on all his fine clothes again and walked off. And the Tigers were very, very angry, but still they would not let go of each other's tails.

And they were so angry that they ran round the tree, trying to eat each other up, and they ran faster and faster, till they were whirling round so fast that you couldn't see their legs at all.

When Ramita saw the melted butter, wasn't she pleased! "Now," said she, "we'll all have pancakes for supper!"

So she got flour and eggs and milk and sugar and butter, and she made a huge big plate of the most lovely pancakes. And she fried them in the melted butter which the Tigers had made, and they were just as yellow and brown as little Tigers.

And then they **all** sat down to supper. And Ramita ate Twenty-seven pancakes, and Kapaali ate Fifty-five, but Little Rajani ate a Hundred and Sixty-nine, because he was so hungry.

How the Turtle Got Its Shell

TALES FROM AROUND THE WORLD

Hello! I am Professor Terry Pin. Today I shall attempt to answer a question as tough as a turtle's shell: How *did* the turtle get its shell?

Turtles appear in legends all around the world. In fact, some people used to believe the world rested on the back of a giant turtle!

One story from China says the universe is
a turtle—and the starry sky is on the inside
of its enormous shell!

But now it is time to hear some stories that
explain how the shell came to be.

Our first tale is from the Algonquian Native Americans.

A long time ago, a handsome, clever god named
Glooskap visited his uncle. Uncle was very kind
but lonely. He couldn't find anyone to marry him.

Glooskap decided to help him. He said, "Wear my clothes to the dance tonight and you will be as handsome as I am."

Uncle did as Glooskap suggested and, sure enough, the chief's most beautiful daughter fell instantly in love with him. This made all the other men very angry!

They got even angrier when Uncle and the chief's daughter got married!

Glooskap knew trouble was brewing. "The men will try to get revenge tomorrow," he warned Uncle after the wedding. "But you can escape by jumping over the lodge. You will jump once, then twice, but the third time will be hard for you. Yet this must be."

The next day, Uncle looked up at the tall lodge with its smoking chimney. How could he possibly jump over it? Yet, when the men approached him, Uncle magically jumped over the lodge. Then he jumped over it again. But the third time . . .

Uncle got stuck on the poles of the chimney. Ouch! They were hot!

Thanks to Glooskap, Uncle survived. His back became a hard shell with smoky marks. Uncle was now a turtle!

But Uncle was still not safe. "The men will try to get you again," Glooskap warned. "You must convince them to throw you in the lake, because there you will be safe."

So Uncle pretended he was scared of the water and the mean men threw him right in!

And there, Uncle lived a long and happy life as a turtle, safe in his shell!

The next story is set in ancient Greece.

The god Hermes loved to play the harp. But the only animal that enjoyed his sweet music was the slow, shell-less turtle.

One day, as Hermes played, he was stung by a bee. "Ouch!" said Hermes, dropping his harp.

The harp landed right on the turtle's back! Hermes decided to reward his loyal fan. He allowed the turtle to keep the harp as a shell that would protect him forever.

Here is my favorite story. It's the one my parents told me when I was little.

Long ago, when the world was new, the Creator gave each animal something to make it special. Some got sharp teeth or claws. Others got horns, stingers, or fins.

But by the time the slow turtle arrived, the Creator's box of Special Stuff was empty, and he was taking his lunch break!

The turtle sighed. "Now I'll never be special," he said to the Creator. "And I'm so slow I probably won't even survive."

"Of course you'll survive," the Creator said kindly. Then he put his empty soup bowl on the turtle's back. "You shall have a shell for protection so you won't need to be fierce or fast. With this shell you can be slow and safe forever."